One day, in the valley, there was not much grass around.
So the goats decided they would cross to higher ground.

"I'll go first," said Little Will, and merrily he ran.
Then Sid jumped out from below —
he turned to Will and sang,

"I don't want beef.
I don't want pork.
I want some goat
upon my fork!"

Said Will, "I'm no good to eat,
but if goat is your prize,
talk to my Big Brother, Bill,
about some Goat Surprise!"

"OK," said Sid, "I'll talk to Bill,"
and let you go onto the hill.

"I'll go next," said Brother Bill, and merrily he ran.
Then Sid jumped out from below —
he turned to Bill and sang,

"I don't want apples.
I don't want prunes.
I want some goat
upon my spoon!"

Said Bill, "I'm no good to eat, but if goat is your prize,
       talk to my brother, Rough Tough Gruff,
       about some Goat Surprise!"
OK," said Sid, "I'll let you pass."

And Bill crossed over to the grass.

"Time for me,"
said Rough Tough Gruff,
so fast and fierce he ran.

So the three goats made their home,
on the green, grassy hill.
And with a munch, they had their lunch,
Rough Tough Gruff and Bill and Will.